Peek!
A Thai Hide-and-Seek

Minfong Ho   illustrated by Holly Meade

CANDLEWICK PRESS
CAMBRIDGE, MASSACHUSETTS

"Jut-Ay, Baby, peek-a-boo,
Want to play? Where are you?"

"Jut-Ay, peek-a-boo,
Oh, hi, dragonfly, is that you?
Stop that tickling in my ear.
Is my baby hiding here?"

Eechy-eechy-egg,
eechy-eechy-egg!

"Jut-Ay, peek-a-boo,
Red-tailed rooster, so it's you!
Flap your wings in the cold dawn air.
Is my baby somewhere near?"

"Jut-Ay, peek-a-boo,
    Oh, puppy dog, it's just you!
    Sniff behind that rattan chair.
    Is my baby crouching there?"

Thoom-thoom, thoom-thoom!

"Jut-Ay, peek-a-boo,
Green-backed turtle, so it's you!
Dive beneath the water clear.
Is my baby splashing here?"

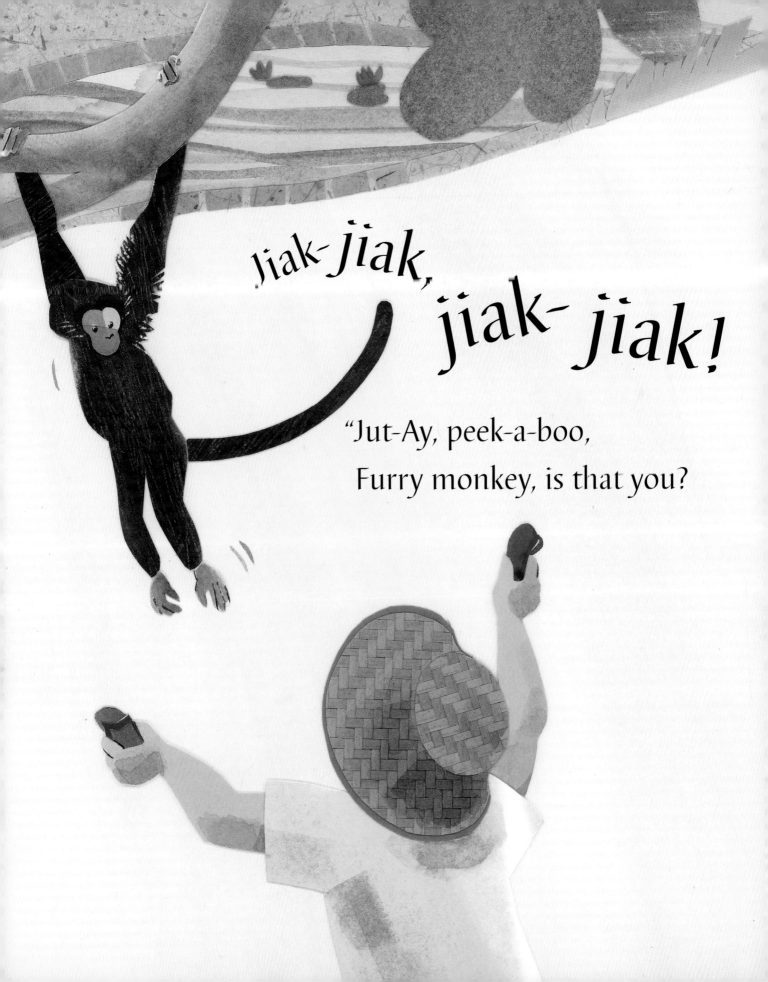

Jiak-jiak, jiak-jiak!

"Jut-Ay, peek-a-boo,
Furry monkey, is that you?

Perched up high in the banyan fair.
Is my baby swinging there?"

Gok- *gok,*
gok-
gok!

"Jut-Ay, peek-a-boo,
Oh, hornbill, so it's you!

Stop that drilling so I can hear
If my baby's somewhere near."

"Jut-Ay, peek-a-boo,
Slithery snake, it's only you—
Coiled behind the orchid rare,
Watching with that glinty stare."

"Jut-Ay, peek-a-boo,
Oh, elephant, so it's you!
Lift the flap of your floppy ear.
Is my baby hiding there?"

Krome-kram,
krome-kram!

"Jut-Ay, peek-a-boo,
Lazy crocodile, it's just you!
What a smile you have, what a sneer.
I hope my baby's nowhere near."

"Jut-Ay, peek-a-boo,
Bright-striped tiger, so it's you!
Did you lure her to your lair?
Did you eat her up in there?"

"Jut-Ay, Papa, peek-a-boo!
Here I am. . . ."

"I found you!"

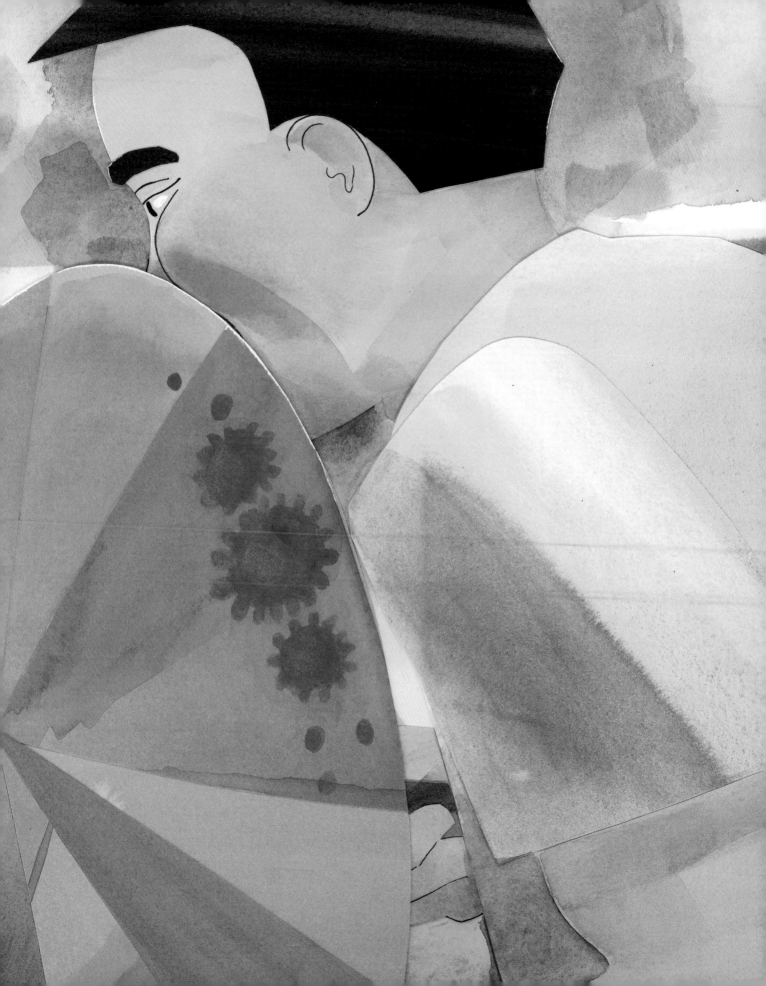

For Chiranan Pitpreechai,
poet, teacher, mother, activist,
gardener—and good friend
M. H.

Text copyright © 2004 by Minfong Ho
Illustrations copyright © 2004 by Holly Meade

First edition 2004

Library of Congress Cataloging-in-Publication Data
Ho, Minfong.
Peek! : a Thai hide-and-seek / Minfong Ho ; illustrated by Holly Meade. — 1st ed.
p. cm.
Summary: A father and daughter play hide-and-seek in the midst of the animals near their house in Thailand.
ISBN 0-7636-2041-6
[1. Hide-and-seek—Fiction. 2. Fathers and daughters—Fiction. 3. Animals—Fiction.
4. Thailand—Fiction. 5. Stories in rhyme.] I. Meade, Holly, ill. II. Title.
PZ8.3H643Pe2004
[E]—dc22   2003055835

2 4 6 8 10 9 7 5 3 1

Printed in China

This book was typeset in Barbedor.
The illustrations were done in watercolor and cut paper collage.

Candlewick Press
2067 Massachusetts Avenue
Cambridge, Massachusetts 02140

visit us at www.candlewick.com

12-04

E   Ho, Minfong
     Peek!

GAYLORD RG